Library of Congress Cataloging in Publication
Number: 2017936249

ISBN: 978-1-68369-010-8

Printed in China

Typeset in Miller and Futura

Story adapted by Jim Thomas
Designed by Doogie Horner
Production management by John J. McGurk

Quirk Books
215 Church Street
Philadelphia, PA 19106
quirkbooks.com

10 9 8 7 6 5 4 3 2 1

E.T.

THE EXTRA-TERRESTRIAL

based on the film written by Melissa Mathison
and directed by Steven Spielberg

illustrated by Kim Smith

It was the week before Halloween.
Elliott wanted to play with his brother Michael,
but Michael said no.

"Come on, guys!" Elliott pleaded.
"I can fight goblins, too!"

"Just go get the pizza," Michael said.

Elliott went outside and paid the deliveryman.

On the way back inside, he heard a noise coming from the shed.

Elliott lived near a forest.
Sometimes coyotes wandered into the shed.
But these footprints didn't look like coyote tracks.

And coyotes don't
roll balls to kids.

It definitely wasn't a coyote.

Elliott tried to tell his family.
"There's a goblin in the shed. A real goblin!"

"Where's the pizza?" Michael asked.

No one believed Elliott's story.

The next day, Elliott went beyond the shed and into the woods to look for the goblin. He saw people with strange equipment, searching for something.

Were they looking for the goblin, too? If they found it, what would they do to it? Elliott had to find the goblin first.

That night, after everyone was asleep, Elliott
left a trail of candy from the shed into the house,

up the stairs,

and into his room.

It turned out the goblin liked candy.

The next day, Elliott introduced the goblin to Michael . . .

And to his little sister, Gertie.

Michael and Gertie quickly realized
what Elliott had learned the night before—
the goblin was kind and very smart.

The kids were excited and curious about their new friend. He seemed too nice to be a goblin.

"Maybe he's a monkey," said Michael.

"I don't like his feet," said Gertie.

"We are here. Home," Elliott said. "Where are you from?"

The goblin pointed
up at the sky!

Then he used his powers
(and some fruits and
vegetables) to create a
model of his solar system.

The goblin wasn't a goblin at all.
He was an extra-terrestrial—
an alien from another planet!
Elliott called him E.T. for short.

Meanwhile, the people looking
for E.T. were getting closer . . .

The next morning, the kids went off to school. Their mom was leaving for work and she heard a noise coming from the closet.

But when she opened the door, all she saw were stuffed animals.

After she left, E.T. had the house all to himself.
He went exploring.

First he made friends
with the local wildlife.

Then he got something to eat.

He found a toy to play with . . .

and something to read.

He watched the television . . .

and learned about Earth forms
of communication . . .

all of which gave him an idea.

If only he could find
everything he needed.

When Gertie came home, she taught E.T. the
alphabet. "B is for balloon," she said.

"B . . ." E.T. said.

"Yes!" Gertie said. "B! Good!"

Elliott got home not much later and
found E.T. in his closet. Gertie and E.T.
were playing dress-up together.

"Elliott . . ." E.T. said.

"I taught him to talk!" Gertie bragged.

Elliott found the box of items that E.T. had collected. He cut himself on a saw blade. "Ouch!" Elliott yelped.

"Ouch," E.T. said. His finger began to glow. E.T. touched his fingertip to Elliott's— and the cut healed!

Then E.T. showed Elliott and Gertie a drawing of something he wanted to build. It looked like a radio. "Phone home," E.T. said.

E.T. worked on his
radio all night.

Meanwhile, the people
who were looking for E.T.
were getting even closer.

E.T. wanted his family to find him and take him home.

But he had to hurry. E.T. wasn't meant to live on Earth.
He was starting to feel sick.

The next day was Halloween. It was the perfect time to get E.T. into the woods, where he could use the radio to send a clear signal home. Michael and Elliott pretended that E.T. was Gertie.

Off they went, into the streets in broad daylight.
No one suspected a thing!
Some of the costumes made E.T. think of home.

Away from other trick-or-treaters,
Elliott and E.T. got on Elliott's bike
and headed into the woods.

When the ride got too bumpy, E.T. took over. Together they rose off the ground and soared through the sky!

They landed in a clearing
and assembled the radio.

E.T. pointed it toward the sky,
and they sat down to wait.

Elliott woke up cold the next morning.
He and E.T. had been in the woods all night!

By the time they got home, the people who were searching for E.T. were at Elliott's house. They were scientists, and they wanted to learn about E.T. They put him in a box to bring him to their lab.

As Elliott was saying goodbye, E.T.'s chest started to glow.

"E.T. phone home!" E.T. said.

"Does this mean they're coming?" asked Elliott.

"Yes!" said E.T.

Elliott knew this was his last chance to help E.T.

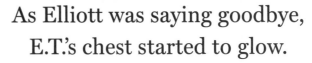

While the scientists were busy packing up their equipment, Elliott and Michael snuck E.T. out of the house.

Michael's friends brought their bikes, and they all raced to the woods.

The scientists chased them!

To escape, E.T. used his powers again,
and all the boys soared up into the sky.

When they reached the forest,
a giant spaceship was landing!

Elliott was sad that his friend had to go.
E.T. was sad, too. The tip of E.T.'s finger lit up,
and he touched Elliott's forehead.

"I'll be right here," said E.T.

Elliott knew he would always remember
their extraordinary friendship.